PUFFIN B

JUSTIN STRIK

Bernard Ashley has had a long career in the teaching profession. As a young teacher in Kent, he taught children with special learning difficulties, and it was from this experience that he saw the need for direct reading matter which would interest older children, so he began writing his own books. He lives in Charlton, South London, not far from the scenes of his early childhood, writing books for children of all ages, from picture books to teenage novels.

Some other books by Bernard Ashley

DINNER LADIES DON'T COUNT
JUSTIN AND THE DEMON DROP KICK
JUSTIN AND THE BIG FIGHT

For older readers

JOHNNIE'S BLITZ
THE PUFFIN BOOK OF SCHOOL STORIES (Ed.)
RUNNING SCARED
THE TROUBLE WITH DONOVAN CROFT

BERNARD ASHLEY

JUSTIN STRIKES AGAIN

Illustrated by Nick Ward

PUFFIN BOOKS

With thanks for some demon ideas to
Ben Armstrong, Oliver Barry, Charlie Childs,
Alistair Goodall and Joel Short of
Christchurch Primary School, London SW3

PUFFIN BOOKS

Penguin Books Ltd, 27 Wrights Lane, London W8 5TZ, England
Penguin Putnam Inc., 375 Hudson Street, New York, New York 10014, USA
Penguin Books Australia Ltd, Ringwood, Victoria, Australia
Penguin Books Canada Ltd, 10 Alcorn Avenue, Toronto, Ontario, Canada M4V 3B2
Penguin Books India (P) Ltd, 11 Community Centre, Panchsheel Park, New Delhi – 110 017, India
Penguin Books (NZ) Ltd, Cnr Rosedale and Airborne Roads, Albany, Auckland, New Zealand
Penguin Books (South Africa) (Pty) Ltd, 5 Watkins Street, Denver Ext 4, Johannesburg 2094, South Africa

On the World Wide Web at: www.penguin.com

Penguin Books Ltd, Registered Offices: Harmondsworth, Middlesex, England

First published 2001
1

Text copyright © Bernard Ashley, 2001
Illustrations copyright © Nick Ward, 2001
All rights reserved

The moral right of the author and illustrator has been asserted

Typeset in 14/22 Palatino

Made and printed in England by Clays Ltd, St Ives plc

British Library Cataloguing in Publication Data
A CIP catalogue record for this book is available from the British Library

ISBN 0–141–30769–2

ONE

'Body behind the ball! Hold it! Take
your time! Look for your man and roll it
out …'

Justin Perfect and his dad were round
behind the garage, goalie-training.
Another shot was volleyed in.

'Two hands to it – don't be so casual.
An' shield it from the runner coming in.'

Justin's dad sat down on the ball. 'I *have*
played in goal before! You're talking
about my best position here. You
concentrate on your own game, striker!'

'Ooooer!' Justin sneered.

But Mr Perfect had had enough of being
shouted at. 'If I'm not good enough you
can get someone else in goal.'

'Would if we could – except I couldn't
play then.' Justin ran up to kick at the

ball. But his dad's backside sort of *overlapped*.

'Ow!'

'Fat lump!'

'That's a foul – *and* verbal abuse.'

'Not a foul!'

'Kicking a ball out of a goalie's hand ...'

'It wasn't in your hand, it was under your b –'

'Same thing.' Mr Perfect gave Justin one of his looks.

'Sorry.' Justin had to be a bit careful. At the school spring fête there were to be Dads' and Lads' and Mums' and Lasses' six-a-side football matches, and Justin's dad was in Justin's team – as goalie. If his dad didn't play then Justin wouldn't either because Simon Lucas fancied *his* dad in goal, and Simon was handy up front as well – where Justin wanted to play.

'No, you're doing all right,' Justin told his dad, going up to him and ruffling his hair as he sat on the ground. 'You'll be ace.'

'Thanks. Anyhow, it must be time for breakfast.' Mr Perfect picked himself up, stretched, and combed his hair back with his fingers. Which left him unready and unguarded as Justin took a last crack at the ball which had rolled out to the penalty spot.

'Yooof!'

'Sorry! Thought you was ready!'

Mr Perfect was ready now. Ready for a limp indoors and a warm sponge.

*

Breakfasts on Saturdays and Sundays were different from the rest of the week because Justin and Miranda's dad was there. Warfare was on hold; cornflakes stayed in bowls and milk went on the cereal instead of over heads.

Mrs Perfect came over from the front

door with an envelope as thin as Kleenex. Justin relaxed. The school didn't send letters in thin white envelopes, theirs were brown and thick. Besides, he hadn't done anything diabolical for days. He forked at his scrambled egg, most of it going into his mouth.

'Oh, it's a letter,' Mr Perfect said.

'Well done, that man!' Miranda could be all-round sarky.

'Who's it from?' her father wanted to know.

But Mrs Perfect had upon her the look of one who knew the answer and dreaded it. The way she'd handed it to her husband had told its own story.

'It's from Dad,' Mr Perfect announced.

'Dad' was Mr Perfect's dad, Grandad Sam, who'd gone to Australia when Justin was born. Not *because* he was born, although some would have thought that reason enough, but because his wife had died and he'd gone out there to start a new life. After a while, he had re-married, but now his second wife had died too. This much the children knew. What they didn't know was what had happened since, something Mr and Mrs Perfect had been talking about in private.

'He's coming back,' Mr Perfect stated.

Mrs Perfect nodded, like a prisoner in

the dock receiving the sentence she'd been told to expect.

'Can he bring a kangaroo?' Justin asked. 'They don't half kick – good for goalie-training …'

Mr Perfect groaned. 'He's coming here, to live with us …'

'Here?' Miranda asked.

Mr Perfect nodded, still reading the letter.

'Where?'

'I said, *here*.'

'I heard that, but *where* here – which room? In the garage?' Miranda persisted. 'We're not a hotel, we haven't got guest rooms. You've got yours, Face-ache's got his, and I've got mine.'

Now Mrs Perfect came into it. She must have had all this sorted in her mind from the early warnings weeks ago.

'He's not coming as a guest, he's

coming as a … as a member of the family. To live.' And she speeded up for the last bit. 'He's having Justin's bedroom.'

For a second or so the only sound to be heard was that of swallowing: scrambled egg and cold, hard fact.

'Do what?!' Justin exploded. 'Where am I gonna sleep? Up the garden?'

'Hopefully,' Miranda said.

But Justin was too angry to bother with that. His bedroom was his bedroom. It was his kingdom, his place, it had the right shape walls for all his football posters, he had a carpet ideal for Subbuteo, and a PlayStation by his bed for late-night World Cup Finals. His world was sorted.

'*WHAT ABOUT ME?*' he shouted.

'You could sell the boy,' Miranda told her mother.

Mr Perfect looked guilty, like a man with egg on his face. Which he had right now. Justin's, scrambled.

'We thought – in the loft,' he said.

TWO

At school, Justin told Tanya about his grandad and his bedroom. She was soft on him and squeezed his hand when she felt sorry in a way that rang little bells. Ting-a-ling.

'He's coming on Saturday and I'm off up in the loft already. There's the water tank that fills up when someone goes to the lav, and you bump your head on the slopey wooden things.'

'Rafters …'

'Yeah, them an' all.'

'Got a carpet?'

'Mats.' Which could have been cow-dunged straw, the way he said it. 'And you have to go up this loft ladder …'

'Rainy days! Tough, Justin.' And she squeezed his hand.

But he was too upset to feel the benefit.

Grandad Sam arrived on the Saturday morning. Justin pretended he had a game of football on and went to the park to kick out his frustration on a ball.

There hadn't been much time for making his loft the snug den they'd promised. His bed had been got in through the dormer window, the mats had been put down, and his things were in a couple of trunks until his dad could get up there and build the units he promised. All right, plaster-board walls had gone up to make it a room instead of a roof space, but Justin couldn't be bothered to pin up his posters, he was too upset. And if Miranda bumped into the loft ladder once more and complained to Justin about it as if it were *his* fault, he'd thread her in and out of the rungs, he swore.

In the park, he kicked his ball hard and hit somebody's dog.

'Watch it, son!'

'Wassup? Is he blind?'

'Yes.'

And there was no answer to that, the way there was no answer to anything these days.

And why did people have to grin all over their faces at visitors – like they were new babies? Then sit listening to them so hard and laughing so much at their stupid jokes? Especially when they weren't

visitors, anyway, but *family*, going to be there for ever?

Grandad Sam sat in Mr Perfect's armchair in the living room as if he were a king on his throne. Round him sat the family like a squad clustered round a football manager. It made Justin feel sick! The old man had arrived, gone to his room, dumped his suitcase and come out to take the star seat in the living room.

Right now he was going on about the weather he'd left behind: cold. 'But you know what they say –'

'What?' asked Justin, itching to speed him up to a finish.

'They say, if you don't like the weather in Melbourne, just wait a coupla minutes!' Grandad Sam laughed, as if he'd cracked the best joke going.

'Why's that?'

'Well, boy, it changes all the time …'

'It does here too.'

'Sure, an' it does in Melbourne.'

'I bet it changes more here than it does in Mel –'

'Justin – leave it!' Mrs Perfect barked. 'What is it about boys?'

'Their bedrooms change every minute – like the bloomin' weather,' said Justin.

He got such a look for that, he thought

he'd better get on to smoother ground.
'You into football down there? Under?' he
asked the old man.

'Australian Rules. Now that's a real
fella's game! Punching the ball about,
plenty of body contact. We're playing it
now. See, we're opposite to you,' he told
Justin, 'your summer here is our winter
there. I had a barbie on Christmas Day …'

'Ooooo! What colour dress?' Justin inquired.

'Barbie. Barbecue, brainless!' Miranda sneered. But before Justin could Australian Rules her to the floor, Grandad suddenly changed the subject.

'Now – I hope you don't take this bad – I'm sure you won't. But I'll come out with it straight. My dear wife's family come from Manchester, and there's a daughter of hers who came out to see us once or twice …'

You could hear the tick of the mantelpiece clock, and that was quartz.

'… So, I wouldn't want to disappoint, but I might settle up there, if – if –'

'If you don't like it here?' asked Justin.

'No – not that, just if things don't pan out for some reason or other. But it's a cinch that they will. *Anyhow –*'

Mrs Perfect got up. 'Anyhow, that's

enough of all this. We're looking forward to happy years. Miranda, you can help me with the tea. Justin, you can –'

But Justin had gone – out to the garden to kick his ball about, but only for the look of things, it was really to be on his own, to think.

What, he asked himself, as he booted one over to next door, *what if for some reason or other Grandad Sam didn't like it here? That would mean the old boy would go up north, wouldn't it, and Justin Perfect could put his name on his own bedroom door again. Couldn't he? Wouldn't he?*

Eh?

THREE

The war against Grandad started early
next morning; on Sunday, the day of rest.
Not that there was ever a day of rest for
anyone who came near Justin because
Justin never rested. His whole life was
geared to football; on his PlayStation, on
his floor, out in the garden or up the
park. Restless balls, balls, balls, balls,
balls.

And it was a ball that began the war. A
good hard size-five signed by Charlton
Athletic, too special to use outside. By
half past five – the light came early
through Justin's scrap of curtain at the
dormer window – he was bouncing it
hard and regular on the loft floor, which
was right over his old bedroom, with
nothing of any muffling carpet on it yet.

Bounce, bounce, bouncey-bounce. Bounce, bounce, bouncey-bounce. Then a bit of a rest to let the old boy think it was over, and bounce, bounce, bouncey-bounce. Water torture with a ball instead of water.

He kept it up for over an hour because Justin could keep things up for ever when he wanted to – and if he wanted Grandad to push off up north he *had* to be determined.

By the time the others were up Justin was out in the garden, chipping balls over the birdbath. When he came in for breakfast he expected to see Grandad red-eyed and grouchy.

But, no. 'Never travel without 'em fellas,' he told the family. 'A good set of earplugs. With the jet lag and my pluggies I've had the best night's kip for a week.'

'Bravo!' said Mrs Perfect.

'Erk,' said Justin. But he really meant something else.

This contest, though, was going to be a game of two halves. You haven't lost till the final whistle. The way he'd wage

the war was like a cup tie, Justin
reckoned – which would have to go to
extra time and penalties before he gave
up.

And right now, at the breakfast table, he
thought of a neat way to score, and make
it look like an own-goal.

'You want another cup of tea?' he asked
Grandad.

Mr Perfect swayed to one side, a touch
of light-headedness, steadied himself
with a hand. Mrs Perfect looked as if
she'd got new contact lenses in, ten times
too big. Justin being helpful?

'Thank you, mate, that's handsome …'

Justin took his cup and went to the
counter, fiddled about for a bit and came
back with it. 'There you go.'

'Cheers.' Grandad supped hard – and spat out tea all over the table. 'Great Barrier Reef! It's stone cold!'

Dabbing, mopping, spooning tea out of the sugar bowl ... and Justin with the face of a choirboy about to sing 'All Things Bright and Beautiful'.

'*Justin!*'

'You have it hot?' Justin asked. 'I thought you was opposite. Your hot's our cold, our cold's your hot ...'

'A natural mistake,' Mrs Perfect hurried in with – 'I'll get you a hot one; and Justin, get a new bowl of sugar ...'

Grandad wiped himself down, muttered apologies, but said he couldn't help it, it was a natural reaction to spit out cold tea when you think it's going to be hot. Justin shook his head as he brought a fresh sugar bowl to the table.

'Here you are, Sam, a nice hot one.'

Mrs Perfect placed it before him. Still choking a bit, Grandad spooned in three from the sugar bowl, stirred and supped again.

And straight off spat another stream of tea the length of the table. Hot tea. They all leapt back. Justin went under the tablecloth shouting, 'Every man for himself!'

'*Salt!* That's *salt!*'

'Whoops! Can't do nothing right, can I?' And Justin left the table seconds before Mr Perfect's swipe at him whistled through the air. He turned at the door on his way out – a long way out on his bike – to see Grandad looking at him with a look that said it all.

I know what your game is, Sunshine …

FOUR

Justin told Tanya Power on the Monday
as they dribbled and passed along the
pavement, sharpening up for their Big
Match at the fête. She was always good
for an idea about home warfare; she and
her big brother Tyrone were like two cats
tied by the tails.

'He knows,' Justin said. 'So I've got to
gear it up a bit ...'

'Bed,' Tanya said. 'Bed's a good place
for tricks.'

Justin wanted to know more.

'An apple-pie bed; or a hedgehog
bed ... prickles down where his feet go.'

'Where am I going to get a hedgehog
just like that?'

'A good spiky clothes brush, stupid!'

Justin thought about it. 'What about a

cat, a real one?'

'Would it stay?'

'No – but it might do a wee …'

'That's cruel.'

'Not as cruel as putting me up in the loft! I banged my head on the slopey wooden thing again this morning.'

'The rafter.'

'Yeah, that an' all.'

But bed would definitely be a good

place to strike, Justin thought, and apple pies they had in the freezer. When he got in from school, luck was on his side. Grandad had gone to register himself for a bus pass and his room was empty. With Miranda at her homework, Dad still in the garage under a car and Mum with an eye on *Countdown* on the TV, Justin struck. Sneaking to the freezer, he found a frozen apple pie, family size, and went to

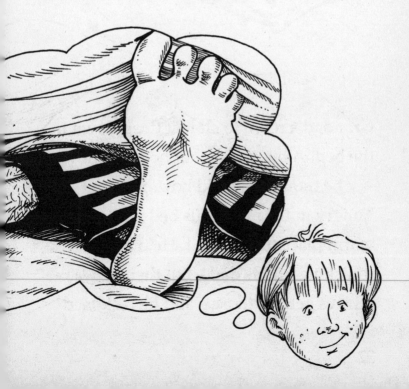

Grandad's room to slide it deep down in
the bed. A bit mega – but he could always
say he thought the old boy might get
hungry in the night. His bed was a good
warm place to defrost it. He'd get a
rollicking off his dad – but then he was
always getting those – and he reckoned

Grandad would definitely start thinking twice about staying.

He couldn't wait for Tuesday morning. He was up and about and teaching the cat to head a ping-pong ball by half past seven.

'Another cracking night's sleep,' Grandad said, coming through to the kitchen. He eyed Justin, a look that said more than 'G'day'. 'Always suffered from hot feet, an' you've come up with the answer.' Mrs Perfect looked puzzled, but she let it rest.

No more said, but something done. Which Justin discovered when he went to bed that night. He climbed up his ladder, got undressed, jumped into bed, slid himself down, and thought for a second that he'd suddenly grown in the day. This was a bed for a titch because his feet could only get halfway down. He could push and push but the bottom sheet was folded back on itself. He had to lie there all night coming out of the top like a jack-in-the-box that's sprung its spring.

And from the landing he thought he heard the sound of laughter. Not his dad's, not his mum's, and not Miranda's. Someone else's, deeper, coming from 'down under'. His Aussie Grandad's …

Usually nothing stopped Justin from being first in the playground to bags the goal against the wall of the boys' outside lavatories. All the other 'goals' were against hall or kitchen windows where you rattled the wire guards if you hit a half-decent shot.

But today Justin wasn't even ready for Tanya when she called at the house. His school jumper was on back to front and he'd got two legs down one hole in his pants. Hopping around at the foot of his loft ladder, he was easy meat for Miranda's shaft of wit.

'Got Drama today?' she asked in her golden-syrup voice. 'Rehearsing the bare-bottomed baboon?'

Justin swung round to hit her and fell over.

'Hey, up you get, mate.' Grandad Sam came out of his bedroom and gave Justin a hand. 'Tired? Not sleep so good?'

Justin said nothing, sorted himself, went downstairs to meet Tanya who was waiting patiently in the porch and told her about his bed.

'*That*'s an apple-pie bed,' she said. 'Folded over like you fold the pastry. It's not a real apple pie you put in …'

And at school he told his best mates the problem.

Of course, they all had grandads they loved to pieces, but with a couple of pushes he got them to understand. There was a rubbing of hands and a smacking of lips. With the best goal gone, they put their minds to some cracking ideas for retaliation, wizard ways to get the old boy running to Manchester for peace and quiet.

'Put a sheep in his bed, Jussy,' said Shaun Newton. 'Tell him it's to remind him of home.'

'Stupid! Where am I going to get a sheep?'

'Never heard of a leg of lamb …?'

'No – phone him from a phone box, put on an upside-down voice and tell him he's left his cooker on and his tap running. Then he'll go home to turn them off.'

'Idiot! He's moved, left the country, migrained to Britain ...'

'Or a shoulder of mutton. That's sheep ...'

'That's rubbish!'

'I've got it!' said Tanya. 'I've got it!'

'Go on!'

'Tell you on the way home ...'

'Is it good?'

'Wait and see ...'

And Justin had to be content with that. But it was enough to get him back to football, scoring a cracking goal that went whistling in past Kojo and through the frame of the hall window, just as it was being opened by the head of Religious Education. (If only he could do that in the Big Match at the school fête!) Unswerving, it carried on a pace and collapsed a display of Love Thine Enemy that she'd been putting up since seven o'clock.

'You hateful, worthless little good-for-nothing!' she screamed at Justin.

Justin bowed to her. She was right – and that was just the spirit he'd got to bring to his war with grandad.

FIVE

Tanya told him on the way home – and he had to say, much as he liked her, he was disappointed. What a build up! What a let-down!

'*Put eggs in his hat?*'

'That's right – then when he puts his hat on, the shells crack and all the yellow runs down his face and his neck, and it dribbles down his back and his chest, and it even goes …'

'Can't do that.'

'Why not?'

'Cos he hasn't got a hat.'

'Then get him one.'

'Don't be daft! Me doshing out for a hat just to spoil it?' In his frustration, Justin kicked a stone on the pavement and chipped the paint on a car door. When

they'd finished running, he told Tanya, 'But he has got slippers, under his bed …'

Indoors, Justin was told that Grandad had gone to join the library – prime time for striking – but Justin went past his door and up to his loft room muttering, 'Homework.'

Mrs Perfect checked with herself – mirror, voice, a pinch of her arm – no, she hadn't died and gone to heaven. Justin – homework? Without being nagged skinny?

But Justin's homework was nothing set by his teacher Mrs de Sousa. He'd set it himself. *Thinking*. He stood looking out of the dormer window at the front then out of the skylight at the back, seeing nothing outside the inside of his own head: going over events. So far, what had gone off between him and Grandad *could* be thought of as accidental. Like some hand balls, up to now it had looked like ball-to-hand, not hand-to-ball deliberate. The apple pie, the cold and salty tea, even the 'mistake' in making Justin's bed – they could all have been proper things that went wrong. Just about. But putting eggs in Grandad's slippers? You couldn't say that was anything except done on purpose. No one kept eggs in slippers under beds, not even big egg-lovers. If he did that, the war would be in the open. Put eggs in those slippers and it was as good as telling the rest of the family he was saying, 'Shove off, cobber!' to Grandad.

Justin prowled the loft room, knocked his head on one of those slopey things and sat on his bed to rub his crown and think some more –

– Only to fall straight through the bed and on to the floor, cracking his backside

a wallop on the thin mat. What the
devil …?

'Are you bouncing balls again?'
Miranda shouted up the loft ladder.

Justin didn't answer. He wasn't going to
admit what he'd just bounced. He pulled
himself up and checked his bed. What
was up with it? The duvet was there, the
pillow was there, the sheets were there.

But what was missing was any sign of a
mattress or a spring – just the outside
framework. His bed had been made up all
stretched tight without the thing that
people lie on – which he now saw stacked
against the dividing chipboard wall.

He was down to the kitchen like a
fireman down a pole.

'Mum! Did you make my bed?'

Mrs Perfect turned from baking her Australian Lamingtons. 'The day you make it no one else will have to! Of course your bed is made.'

'I didn't say "Is it made?" Listen to the words, watch my lips. I said, *"Did you make it?"* Today?'

He nearly got his Lamington there and then, over his head. But Mrs Perfect was

intrigued. 'As it happened, not today. Grandad's been giving me a hand in the house. He went up and made it.'

'And yesterday?'

'And yesterday. Why, do you want a rebate on the rent you don't pay me?'

'No, but …'

She turned back to her chocolate and coconut. And Justin went out of the kitchen. Not towards the telly or his bedroom, though; but to the utility room where such things were kept that they didn't want too warm, yet didn't want fridge cold.

Like eggs.

Right, Aussie Grandad! Open warfare it was!

Next morning, Justin woke to a quiet house – no ranting, no 'Justin!' being shouted from the foot of the loft ladder.

Just the sound of birds singing outside.
He got up and dressed – no time to wash
today – because you had to be ready in
warfare. Soldiers in dug-outs didn't
bother with soap when the enemy was
about. And looking out of the skylight
into the back garden, Justin almost did a
backflip in triumph. There were
Grandad's slippers, pegged on the clothes
line, dripping water.

'Ha!'

He made for his loft ladder, to go down and walk past Grandad without saying a word. And if *he* said anything – if Grandad complained about Justin – then Justin could let on about the no-mattress bed.

But Grandad was sitting and reading the paper in the living room as if nothing whatever was different – except he was in his socks. When Justin hovered in the doorway he looked up and gave him a nod.

'Morning, mate.'

'Wotcha.' Justin looked at the man. He was on the small side, shiny grey hair, a suntanned face, glasses on for the paper – but modern ones. He wasn't really an *old boy* old boy. And as the man looked at Justin, he seemed to have a glint in his eye. Or was it a sparkle? Whichever, he didn't look ready to run off up north just yet.

Anyhow, Justin would be ready tonight for any tricks he wanted to pull …

'Justin – breakfast!' his mother shouted.

'Coming. What is it?'

'Marmite toast, cereal, the usual …'

'Oh. Shame.'

'Shame?'

'I wanted eggs – all squashed up and scrambled ...' Which Justin said to the living room and Grandad, not to the kitchen.

But Grandad continued reading the paper as if he hadn't heard. Perhaps just a little 'Hmmmph' in his throat ...

SIX

At school, Justin had another war on: the football match which was coming up on Saturday. As Mr Anchor was getting out of his Robin Reliant, Simon Lucas started going on at him about who was going to be in their team.

'Sir, my dad's a good goalie – used to play for Greenwich Youth – an' I'm an ace striker. Why's it Perfect and his dad are in the team?'

But Justin was up to that. 'Greenwich Youth? When was that, when they wore woad?'

'Lads, lads …' said Mr Anchor.

'You put "Justin and Mr Perfect" on the team sheet,' Justin said. 'You can't change it just cos Lucas don't like it …'

Mr Anchor fixed him with his

almost-in-control look. 'A headmaster, Justin Perfect, is the king of his castle, the lord of his domain, he who wields power with wisdom. If such a person –'

'You gonna change it then?'

'No I'm not …'

And dusting his hands, Justin walked away.

'… Unless there's a no-show.'

'There won't be,' said Justin. 'We'll be there.'

Which was a result – seeing off Lucas – plus he was giving Grandad as good as he got, doing him over the slippers. So, it was a happy Justin – till lunchtime, when he sat in the canteen with his cronies and bit into his favourite cheese and pickle sandwich.

Soap and pickle! Erk! A big mouthful of it, spat out. With a little bit of paper on the underside of the bread and one word written on it.

'ENJOY.'

Right! So what would it be – that sheep in the bed? Or locking the lavatory door from the inside when Grandad wanted to go and climbing out through the window? Or stretching cling film across the bog seat? Sewing up the bottoms of his pyjama trousers? Sawing halfway through a leg of his bed? Justin went through all the ideas, most of them useless, especially stuff with trip wires and buckets of water over doors. He didn't want him injured, he wasn't a bad old bloke, he was just living in Justin's

room. He wanted him off, away, up north, vamooshed; he could always come to tea …

So, what was he going to do to get his own back big time?

Indoors, he said nothing, put his packed lunchbox on the counter. Grandad said nothing, fiddled outside the back door with a new plug he was putting on the hover-mower, a breeze ruffling his hair.

And that gave it to Justin. That gave him the answer. That told him what he was going to do tonight …

He'd hidden what he needed under the rug on the landing. And he'd set his Casio to buzz him at three a.m. Everyone was always asleep at three a.m., weren't they?

Now his watch buzzed, and at first he wondered what it was buzzing for – until his brain cleared of sleep and he remembered. Tonight he was going to give Grandad the works …

Of course, it was creak, creak, creak, however careful he was; but by thinking fairy steps, fairy steps, fairy steps, Justin went across his floor and down his loft ladder.

Outside Grandad's door he waited, listened. Grandad was snoring full strength in there – hmmmph-guff, hmmmph-guff, hmmmph-guff – had to be Australian Rules snoring. Very carefully, Justin pulled the scissors from under the landing rug, pushed down the handle of Grandad's door as if he were defusing a bomb, and crept into the room, ready to butt straight out. But the old boy was well into the Land of Nod. Hmmmph-guff, hmmmph-guff, hmmmph-guff.

As if on feet borne by ants, Justin

wafted across to the bed. Grandad looked
so peaceful, with his shiny grey hair
smoothed out on the pillow like a baby's.
And it was only a matter of moments to
snip, snip, snip it away. Scary work, but
so good to do.

'Wha's that?' There was a grinding

of teeth and the old boy suddenly stirred.

Justin crouched fast. He could always say he was looking for a Subbuteo man he'd lost, anything to get him out of the room.

Then, hmmmph-guff, hmmmph-guff, hmmmph-guff; Grandad went off again.

And as Justin crept out of the room, he snorted at a wicked thought. He'd clipped old Grandad like a shearer. From now on he wasn't Grandad Sam but Grandad Shaun!

SEVEN

Back up in his loft, the full strength of what he'd done suddenly hit him. Even Justin Perfect could see that it was diabolical! Grandad couldn't remake his hair like he could remake an apple-pie bed, he couldn't hang his hair out on the line to dry like he had his slippers; he'd got to live with it, wait for it to grow. The family would see it, point at it, talk about it. This time Justin had definitely gone over the top – for which he'd get into mega trouble. He probably wouldn't get another Christmas or birthday present till he was in line for his old age pension. When they saw Grandad's head Justin's mum and dad would come storming up his loft ladder like attackers up the ramparts.

So Justin pulled it up, closed the trap door and slid his clothes chest across the top of it. Now they couldn't get to him. After they'd all cooled down a bit, when they thought he was fainting with hunger, they might feel a bit sorry for him – that was his only chance.

'Justin! Justin! School …' his mother shouted up from the kitchen.

Be deaf, he thought. It was too soon for them to start feeling sorry for him. But the trouble suddenly was, it wasn't too soon for something else. It's not just feeling hungry or thirsty that turns a hiding place into a prison – there's that pesky need to go to the lavatory. That's what gets people coming out.

'Tanya's been and gone! Come down, will you?' His mother was on the landing now. 'Let down this ladder!'

No way! But by half past eight Justin

was hopping about desperately wanting the bathroom: no vases, no bottles, no old tin helmets up in their loft. He thought about using the water tank, but even he couldn't bring himself to do that. People washed in that water!

Knock, knock, knock, knock, knock. There was the sudden heavy rap of a broomstick on the trap door. 'Justin! Get this ladder down!' His father had come in from the garage.

Oooo! By now Justin was crossing his legs, clutching himself. Them feeling sorry for him would take hours, but this he could feel happening any second.

'What stupid game is this?'

No one had mentioned Grandad. The bit of Justin that thought cool and gave him his edge told him that no one was going on about *hair*. It was just him and school and Tanya they'd gone on about up to now … So if Grandad was having a lie-in, perhaps he could get out of the house before anyone blew 'Foul!'

Anyway, Justin *had* to go.

He slid the chest off the trap door, opened up and let the ladder go – the smooth aluminium slid to the landing and whacked Mr Perfect a nasty one on the shoulder.

'Ow! You stupid boy! Give warning!'

'Ladder ho!'

'It's too late now!' Mr Perfect was walking round and round in tightening circles, clutching at his shoulder.

But, running for the bathroom, Justin's sympathy was feeble. 'Daft place to stand,' he told him.

When he came out there were two main bits of news. One, there was no sign of Grandad; his bedroom door was open, his bed was made, and he was nowhere to be seen. Two, his father's right arm was in a sling. Nothing broken, they reckoned, but he was definitely out of Saturday's football match at the fête.

Dog-muck luck! Which meant that Justin was out of it as well. Grim and glum he walked late to school, ready to give Mrs de Sousa the sort of day she'd never forget. But he wasn't saying anything to Simon Lucas. The one thing in the world he didn't want to see was Lucas smiling and punching the air in triumph.

He slouched across the playground, stamped up the stairs, pushed into the classroom and kicked his way past careless feet to his seat. 'Wotchit!' he told the world.

'Ah, Justin,' Mrs de Sousa said. 'You're here.'

The scraped chair, the banged table, the slammed books, the growled threats told them all that Justin was indeed there – and they should all watch out.

So why was Mrs de Sousa looking sugary like Glynda, the kind Wizard of Oz witch?

'We're all so sorry ...' She was speaking

as if for the whole of the class – who were
wondering what they were all so sorry
for.

Her voice went croaky crestfallen.
'Justin – this sad letter from home – I
know why you're late and you shan't
have an "absent" mark …'

As if Justin cared!

'… I must share it, if you don't mind –
so your classmates can understand why

you might be "down" today ...' Demons could invade Mrs de Sousa as well. Not once in the whole year had she had a chance like this ... She opened an envelope and took from it a sheet of thin air-mail paper.

'"Dear Teacher,"' she read to the class,

'"Please be big-hearted towards Justin Perfect today. He has lost the cuddly kangaroo he takes to bed each night to help him off to sleep, his little Roo-Roo as he calls it …"'

Already the class was cracking up, and Mrs de Sousa was fighting to keep the smile off her face with a mouth that was going all ways. Justin was glaring ahead, he couldn't believe his ears.

'"… He's looked everywhere, in his toy box, in his Noah's Ark and in his dolls' house. It has vamooshed, and he cried himself to sleep last night. His last shot is that he might have given it away with Bub-Bub his bunny to Mary-Lou, his little friend next door. Please make due allowances for a mega upset young fellow.

'"Yours sincerely, S. Perfect."'

'Aaaah!' said Mrs de Sousa.

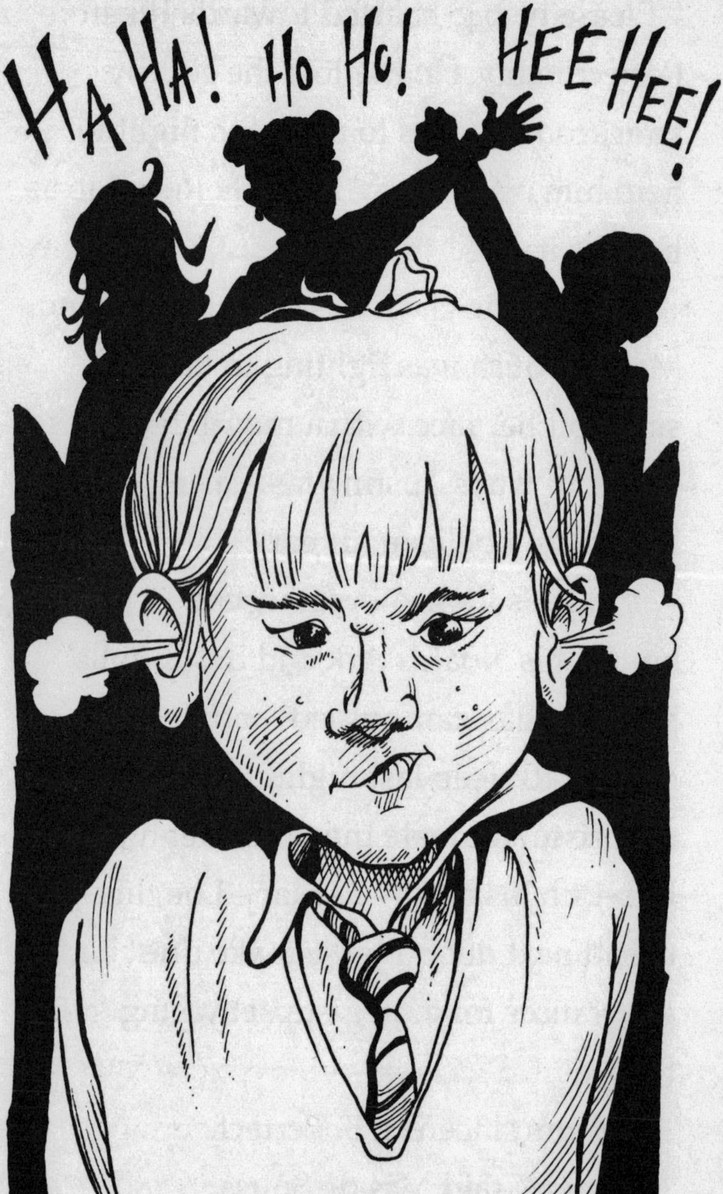
HA HA! HO HO! HEE HEE!

'Aaaah!' said the class, a second before they fell about, thrashing the air with helpless arms and kicking the floor with hysterical feet. So many of them, in all directions, that Justin didn't know where to lash out first.

So he sat there, lips like sewn-up prunes, and stared at the red face and bobbling throat of Mrs de Sousa.

One up for her, and one up for Grandad – no, a million up for Grandad. A cracking goal – Roo Roo and Bub-Bub would stick like Pritt.

But in the playground, Justin got a surprise. At break, the others let him off the hook. Where he reckoned he'd be chasing people round the yard teaching them some respect, instead they started giving him acclaim for having such a great grandad. They'd had their laugh, now came their envy.

'My grandad's boring!' said Tanya. 'What a load of fun yours is ...'

'Cracking!' said Kojo. 'Jussy's grandad's ace!'

And it was true, when Justin thought about it. Sam Perfect was very different from most grandads you heard about. Taking so much trouble to get his own back.

'Lucky devil!' said Simon Lucas.

Simon Lucas – who was the only person to bring Justin down again. Too right, Justin had got a grandad to make them all jealous. But he hadn't got a dad who was fit to play in the Dads' and Lads' game this Saturday ...

When Justin got home that afternoon, Grandad was out of the house again – but in a big way. He wasn't coming back for a day or so.

'Where's he gone?'

'About his business,' Mrs Perfect said.
'He's been acting a bit odd, I must say.
Had a short haircut, packed a bag, and
went ...'

And Justin knew where, he reckoned.

Up north. So he'd won the war after all, and the letter to school had been Grandad's last shot.

Which was a bit of a shame after all the acclaim he'd had …

And how could a winner celebrate getting his room back when he was brought down over the Dads' and Lads' match? The having to be there – they were giving out the season's football medals – and him not getting in the big game because of his dad's injury.

Justin Perfect's world had definitely gone very squashed bananas.

EIGHT

'Right, teams!' shouted Mr Anchor, after a FIFA blast on his whistle. He was in his Charlton away top and a pair of shorts for refereeing.

'Fancy his wife letting him wear shorts with those legs!' one of the mothers said.

'He can wear 'em for me!' said a gran. 'My favourite colour, blue.'

'Them shorts are red ...'

'I'm talking about his legs!'

Mr Anchor shivered on bravely. 'Teams – who's here?!'

Well, Simon Lucas definitely was, he'd been working his dad closer and closer through the throng to Mr Anchor from the moment he'd seen Justin's dad with his arm in a sling.

And Justin was there, looking in a foul

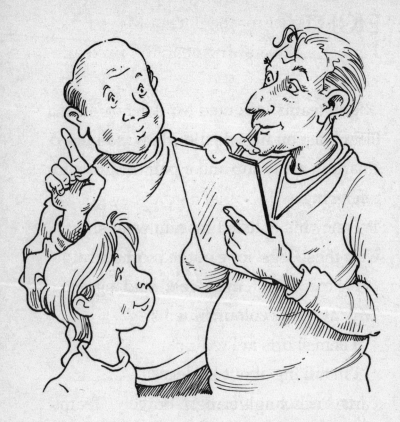

mood. He'd already sent Eddie Mason to the First Aid tent on account of a misguided song about 'Roo Roo roo the boat gently down the stream …' Now he was going to have to watch Mr Anchor substitute Mr Lucas for Mr Perfect in goal.

'Goalkeeper for the Blues – Mr Perfect …?' read Mr Anchor off his team sheet.

Simon and Mr Lucas elbowed forward. They both cleared their throats and leaned towards the headteacher, allowing just a moment's polite quiet before they got Mr Perfect scratched off the team sheet.

Except,'Here y'are, mate,' suddenly came a voice from the back of the crowd. Was Mr Lucas a ventriloquist?

'Where?' asked Mr Anchor.

'Over here – I'm Mr Perfect.' A figure came threading through.

Justin stared. It was Grandad, with a 'number one' haircut!

Mr Anchor looked from Justin to Justin's dad to Justin's grandad. While Simon Lucas piped up, 'That's not Mr Perfect –'

'It fair dinkum is! Wanna see the papers?' Grandad rasped. He was dressed in a football top, tracksuit trousers with a pair of shiny new Adidas football boots. 'Sam Perfect,' he said, grasping Mr Anchor's hand and nearly shaking him off over the heads of the crowd. 'Jussy's grandad. Nothin' wrong with that, is there?'

'No, no, no, no, no,' replied Mr Anchor. 'You're in goal for Blues. Have a good game.' And he moved on to check the rest of the teams.

'Get changed, mate,' Grandad told Justin. 'Get them shooting boots on.'

Justin jumped as Grandad threw his boots at him – boots he'd brought from home, the dear, kind old cobber ... And he'd called him *Jussy* – like his mates did.

'Grandad! Here!'

But that shout wasn't just Justin, it was all the team when Grandad had the ball.

They adopted him straight off as one of their own. The lads knew how cracking he was, and the dads could see he knew what he was about in goal.

He needed to be good. It was a tough old game. Dads from one side tackled lads from the other with no allowance for age or size – once that match ball starts bouncing the will to win runs on wheels of fire.

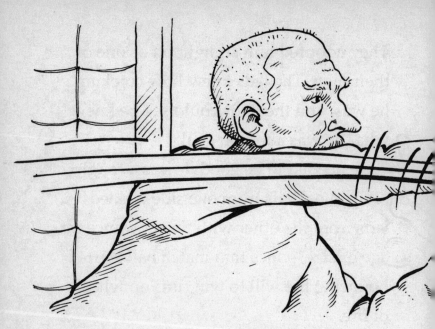

Justin played his best, but he was
bundled off the ball as soon as ever he got
it. And Grandad saw plenty of action
because the Reds were getting more shots
at goal. He dived left, he dived right, he
reached high and he reached wide, he
came out to feet and scooped the ball
bravely away from the biggest dads in the
world – but it was what he did with it
once it was in his arms that had everyone
shouting for him.

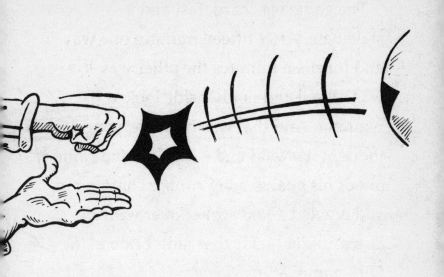

He put the ball on the flat of his left
hand, swung back his right like a boxer
winding up for a knock-out, and punched
the ball with his fist to send it screaming
to the other end of the pitch. Australian
Rules style – hard, fast and deadly
accurate.

'Wooof!' shouted the crowd every time.

Nothing got past him, but then nothing
got to Justin past the big defenders on the
other side either.

The game was hard, fast and a stalemate. After fifteen minutes one way and fourteen minutes the other way it was nil–nil and neither side looked like winning. And that was how everyone thought it would end – till Grandad came out of his goal to a big runner charging in and bowled a Red striker over with a down-under tackle that didn't rate in the FIFA game.

Whistle. 'Foul!' shouted Mr Anchor. 'Penalty!'

Grandad grimaced. He never argued with referees, of course.

Everyone watched, knowing the outcome, knowing the final result, one–nil to Reds, as the shot was set up. Mr Strong, the dad who'd been brought down, fought off the rest of the lads on his side to take the penalty himself. This was going to be the winning kick, no doubt

about it. He placed the ball, paced back
ten metres – it was going to sear past
Grandad, tear a hole in the net and power
across the school field into the hedge –
and started his run up for the kick.

But Justin knew this dad's lad. He knew
what Barry Strong did at penalties – and
Barry had to have been taught by Mr

Strong, didn't he? Just as the man was a stride away from kicking the ball, too late to change his tactic, Justin suddenly yelled at Grandad.

'Low left!'

Without hesitation, Grandad went – low left – as Mr Strong struck the ball: low right, from his end of things. Pow! The ball went scudding goalwards, straight into the safe hands of Grandad Perfect, who seemed to be down there waiting for it.

Wow! What a save! The claps! The cheers! But the goalie from down under wasn't finished – and he wasn't hanging about. With a somersault he was on his feet, rolling the ball in front of him out of the penalty area and charging, dribbling through the other side to the other end of the pitch. Australian Rules allow more body contact, and they all got that. Wallop! Bounce! Bump! All fair and to the shoulder, Mr Anchor ruled. No one could get near Grandad, except Justin who was pelting alongside to his right. Two men to beat, one of them turned the wrong way screwing himself into the pitch, and now there was one – and the other goalie.

'Jussy!' Grandad shouted – and with the neatest twist of his foot, he sent the ball to

Justin, who didn't need telling what to do. With a sweet, accurate instep from his gifted right foot, Justin met the ball first time and sent it cracking across the short grass and deep into the other net.

'Goal!'

'One–nil!'

And, after the final whistle from Mr Anchor – 'We won! We won! We won!'

Justin turned to shake Grandad's hand. What a solo effort! What a final pass! What a shot! But Grandad wasn't there. Sam Perfect was being carried shoulder high by two dads and their lads across the pitch to where the trophy cup was set on a table to be awarded.

What a save! What a run! What a game! What a grandad!

They walked home together, Justin and Grandad, leaving Mr and Mrs Perfect and

Miranda to go round the stalls. Not much was said because there didn't seem much *to* say, actions had been so much louder than words. Except, where had Grandad been the last few days? What had he been up to, going away and coming back? Which became clear at a turning a few streets short of Justin's house.

'Come down here, mate ...' Grandad
suddenly said. It was a quiet cul-de-sac of
smallish bungalows. 'When I went for my
bus pass, and my library books, and my
haircut –' Grandad rubbed his cropped
head – 'I wasn't just on the one track,
mate ...'

'No?'

'I was taking a squint at this place.'
Grandad stopped outside a neat little
bungalow with an overgrown garden and
a For Sale sign. 'What do you reckon
to it?'

Justin looked. A place was a place,
wasn't it? What was he supposed to say?
Then the brain switched from his feet to
his noddle.

'It's fair dinkum,' he said, smiling.

'Well, I like being near you lot, plenty of
life,' Grandad told him. 'Reckon I might
stick about – but I feel bodger about
turfing you out of your room ...'

'No –' Justin started.

'So I've put a deposit down on this.
Went walkabout up to London for a
coupla days, sorted out my money ...'

'But you don't have to move,' Justin
finished. And he meant what he said next.
'You stay with us, I like it up my loft.'

Grandad Sam ruffled his hair. 'You're the apples an' rice, a real good 'un, a kid after my own heart. But I won't be far – coupla streets away.'

'Be great!' said Justin. And he found himself doing what he hadn't done since the old man came. He touched him, put his arm in his.

'But don't you ever doze off,' the old man said. 'I ain't *started* yet in the tricks department ...'